Dedicated with all my love to Rafa and Nico, who have lived
together with my spooky ghosts while I drew them,
with patience, joy and plenty of kisses.

Haunted Houses Handbook

Text and Illustrations © Mónica Carretero
This edition © 2012 Cuento de Luz SL
Calle Claveles 10 | Urb Monteclaro | Pozuelo de Alarcón | 28223 Madrid | Spain
www.cuentodeluz.com
Original title in Spanish: Manual de Casas Encantadas
English translation by Jon Brokenbrow

ISBN: 978-84-15241-05-8

Printed by Shanghai Chenxi Printing Co., Ltd. October 2012, print number 1325-02

Other stories from the HANDBOOK series:

Mónica Carretero

Haunted Houses Handbook

CUENTO
DE LUZ

Mrs. Peck,
tired of living in the city, decided that she wanted to begin
a new life in a much quieter place, in the countryside next to the sea.
So she set out to find a new house to live in. She looked everywhere.
"They're so expensive!" she thought.
One day, walking along the street with her son and feeling a little sorry for
herself, Mrs. Peck suddenly saw a shop with a sign that read
Haunted House Agency, which rented out Haunted Houses.

"My dear, you've come to the right place!" said the owner of the agency happily.
"The houses I'm going to show you are lovely, and I'm sure we'll find one for the
right price. They really are very, very special houses!"

"I don't know if I want to live in a Haunted House," said Mrs. Peck.
"I don't think it's really the right thing, but we need something
pretty, quiet, and cheap."
"Not the right thing?" asked the owner of the *Haunted House
Agency*. "I'm sure these are just the houses you're looking for, and they'll
be perfect. You and your son will never feel alone.
Don't tell me you're afraid of ghosts? The ones
in these houses are quite harmless, and
you can see right through them.
I'm sure you can trust them all.
I'll give you a few tips you should
bear in mind, and we'll visit some houses.
You can see them from top to bottom,
inside and out, so that when you do decide,
you'll be sure it's the right home for you.
Let's begin!"

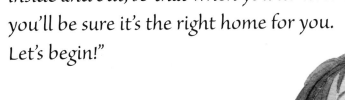

So, what is a Haunted House?

A Haunted House is just a house where ghosts live.
Haunted Houses are usually spooky and abandoned. Ghosts
love to be alone, and for the first few days they do everything
they can to try to get the future tenants to run for their lives,
without looking back and without ever, ever returning.
That's why, when we see someone running really fast, we say
they look like they've seen a ghost!
Ghosts like peace and quiet.
After all, they were there first!

But there are also Haunted Houses that are absolutely lovely, either because there are people living in them, or because their ghosts take extra special care of them. Here we can see an example of ghosts and people living together in perfect harmony. After a couple of months of frights and scares, screams and panic, everything goes back to normal, with everyone living together peacefully.

Note: Only three out of every ten cases like this will actually have a happy ending.

There are **typical things** you can find in every Haunted House. The more you know about them, the quicker you can get used to them.

For example:

1. False mirrors.
2. Objects that come to life.
3. Houses that turn into haunted houses during a full moon.
4. Broken windows with lace curtains blowing in the wind.
5. People running around scared out of their wits.
6. Bells that make scary noises.
7. Photos of former tenants.
8. Secret doors, padlocked doors, suspicious doors, and more doors in all shapes and sizes.
9. Things that go bump in the night.

Types of ghosts

But of course, what every Haunted House
has is at least one ghost.

You can see a few examples in these
photos:

1. Ghosts in paintings.
2. Ghosts who wear sheets.
3. Ghostly shadows.
4. Flesh-and-blood ghosts.
5. Holographic ghosts.
6. Ghosts that appear in windows.

"So now we know whom we might come across in a Haunted House. Now, my dear Mrs. Peck, before we start visiting some houses... Could you and your son tell me how many ghosts are in this room? Take your time, look carefully, and once you've found them all, we can begin our visits."

Solution: There are 14 ghosts and a sleepwalking cat.

"Trembly Manor is the first house we're going to visit. It's in the English countryside, just two days' journey (by horse and carriage) from London. I'm sure, Mrs. Peck, that you'll fall in love with its garden, eight bedrooms, fully equipped kitchen, lounge with three fireplaces, and library full of secret passages. It also has the typical locked attic and basement that you'll never go into, just in case. Trembly Manor has all this, plus coal fires and twelve bathrooms!"

Trembly Manor was wonderful, a dream come true. But from the very first night, Mrs. Peck and her son never slept a wink. All of the beds (in all eight bedrooms!) were too small for them—much too small. They knew that it was very important to get a full night's rest, and so they decided to look for another house. They phoned the owner of the *Haunted House Agency* and set off their search.

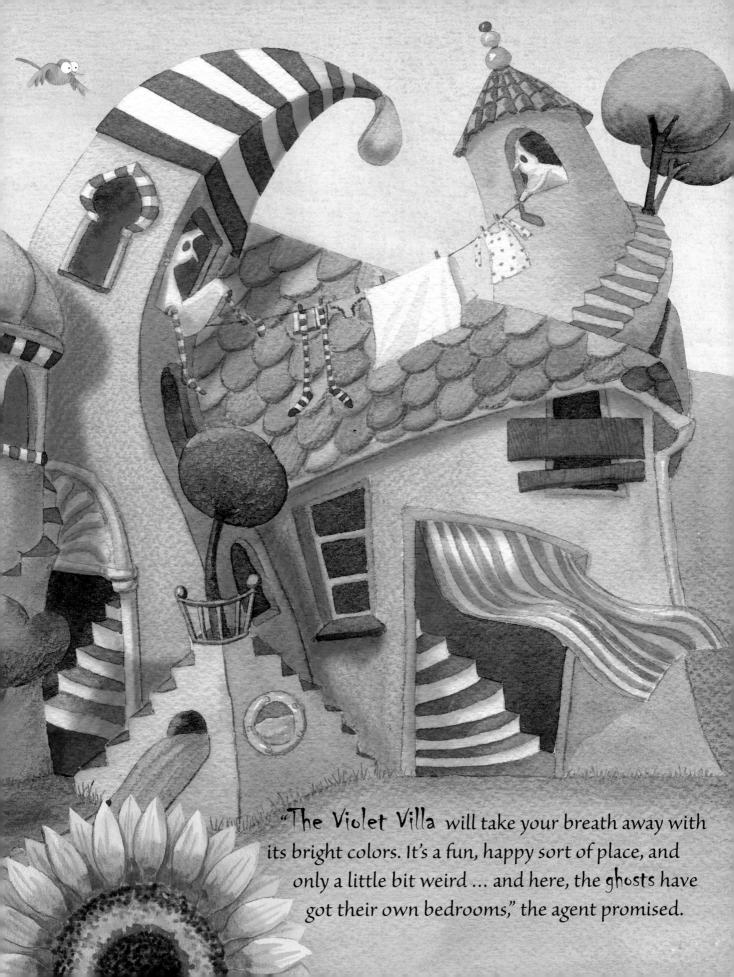

"The Violet Villa will take your breath away with its bright colors. It's a fun, happy sort of place, and only a little bit weird … and here, the ghosts have got their own bedrooms," the agent promised.

Well, the house really did take their breath away ... because they couldn't stop screaming!! Stairs that went up to the floor and came down from the ceiling; doors that opened out onto nothing; endless corridors where they didn't know if they were walking backwards or forwards, up or down ... As soon as they walked through the door of The Violet Villa, they felt positively dizzy. It would have been a great place for a fun fair, but to live in? No way!

"Don't tell me you've never dreamed about living in a castle!" exclaimed the owner of the *Haunted House Agency*. "This is a fine example of a Haunted House where people live together with ghosts. It's been looked after by the DeVille family for centuries. They're such lovely people..."

"Well then, take a look at Quivery Castle," suggested the real estate agent. "Eighteen enormous drawing rooms with tapestries and suits of armor, five pointy towers, dungeons, and a fireplace in every room. Plus, during the last renovation, we even added a bathroom!"

"It's only got one bathroom?" asked Mrs. Peck with alarm.

As it turned out, the living people were scarier than the ghosts! The housekeeper had a long, creepy face, and the butler kept rattling the chains that were attached to his ankles along with an enormous ball on one end. All of the different food they brought to the table talked, winked, or opened and closed its mouth.

"Mom, I think I'd prefer a smaller house!" whispered Mrs. Peck's son, as he tried not to catch the eye of a huge carp that kept staring at him.

"Well, I've left the house I think you'll like the best for last," announced their agent. "It's the Lighthouse Keeper's Cottage, next to the sea on the top of a hill, surrounded by trees and flowers. It's got three bedrooms, a den with a fireplace, a kitchen and dining room, big windows all around, a porch with lovely views of the sunset, two bathrooms, and a ghost pirate who lives with his mother."

"Aha! Two bathrooms! That's perfect," thought Mrs. Peck.

"Yes, honey, this is just right for us," said Mrs. Peck,
full of emotion. She could feel in her heart that she
and her son would be happy there.
"Mom, look! I can see the shadow of the pirate!"

They were so happy in the **Lighthouse Keeper's Cottage!** The ghost pirate turned out to be absolutely charming. Every day he would tell them incredible tales, and his mother was very discrete, as she was a shadow ghost. And she made such wonderful cakes! Mrs. Peck and the pirate got on wonderfully, so much so that they fell in love—but that's another story! And so, in the end, it had been a great idea to visit the *Haunted House Agency* to look for a new house, and to discover that there are very nice ghosts!

Haunted Maze

Find the route that leads Mrs. Peck's son to his friend the ghost.

Word Search

Find seven words connected with the houses that Mrs. Peck and her son visited.

```
c a s t l e l o a i
h r u f a o g k r d
i a r a e m e a m p
m s c n c g s e a e
n m p t a h a r d r
e n e e a o a n u d
y a e s c s c t r o
a r m o r t o a u a
f n c a t o e u a p
e a o l d o g r t o
```

Word search solution: castle, ghost, specter, chimney, armor, cat, dog 7 Differences solution: red flower, flower on the door, fish's fin, dog's tail, dog's nose, teddy bear's nose, mother ghost's foot.

Find the 7. Differences